MW01166106

Ezra's Journal

by James E. Ryhal

Best Wishes
Jim Ryhal

19743

DORRANCE
PUBLISHING CO.
EST. 1920
PITTSBURGH, PENNSYLVANIA 15222

This is a work of fiction. Names, characters, places, and incidents are either the product of the author's imagination or are used fictitiously, and any resemblance to actual persons, living or dead; events; or locales is entirely coincidental.

Dorrance Publishing Co
701 Smithfield Street
Pittsburgh, PA 15222
Visit our website at www.dorrancebookstore.com

ISBN: 978-1-4809-1013-3
eISBN: 978-1-4809-1335-6

To Sonya, the Amazing Grace in my life.

FOREWORD

When I was seven years old, my parents divorced. Consequently, my mother took me and my younger sister and moved from Erie, Pennsylvania, to be with her parents in New Castle, Pennsylvania. My grandmother was a powerful woman, and most of the family gathered around her. On the other hand, I felt more of a desire to be around my grandfather.

My grandfather was a very interesting man. He was a slender 6'1" tall and a very thoughtful individual. In 1912 he finished his studies at The Ohio State University and later studied at an electrical engineering school in Maryland. He seemed to know a great many things about a great many subjects. I enjoyed talking to him about automobile engines, outboard motor engines and any minor technical problems I could understand. Because of my age, my own knowledge was quite limited, but he taught me many things. Most of all, I enjoyed watching him repair things, such as an automobile engine, a clothes washing machine or a lawn mower.

Since I was the one who shared most of the conversations with my grandpa, Harold J. Van Buren, it was only natural that he began to share things about his youth on the farm in central Ohio. He was born in 1890 and was well-acquainted with his grandfather, Ezra Hezekiah Van Buren. Ezra was born in 1842 and died in 1915. Therefore, my grandfather knew him for 25 years. Since he was the oldest child in his family, Harold knew Ezra longer and better than any of his brothers and sisters. This greatly helped me in my preparation for this book because Harold shared many of the stories that Ezra had told him about the American Civil War. A familiar quotation he often repeated was that President Abraham Lincoln often said that Ohio saved the Union.

At first meeting Harold, he didn't talk a great deal; as he grew more familiar with you, he talked a very great deal. As I grew older, I began to appreciate him more and more as a scientist and as a person. It became clear to me that he had shared many long talks with his grandfather Ezra about the War Between the States. Since I became the grandchild that talked to him the most, he told me much about the war, about Ezra and about Ezra's experiences from 1862 to 1865.

Grandpa described Ezra as a man of about six feet. By today's standards, he would not be considered a large man but possessed much physical and mental toughness. As I wrote the rough draft of the book, I could understand how Ezra overcame the obstacles and bad weather during his escape and even ordinary days in the Union Army. He undoubtedly developed many survival skills working and growing up on the family farm.

From my very early days, I remember Harold talking about Libby Prison in Virginia. As a small boy, I had no idea where that was or what it was, but I began to read a lot about that horrific prison. He told me Ezra had never been sick or injured during his time in the army or in Libby Prison. I can guess that he developed physical strength and resistance to illnesses from his work and life on the farm. In our conversations, he always spoke of Ezra in strong and complimentary terms. I wondered if my grandfather ever grew tired of my inquisitiveness about Ezra, but it appeared that he never did. I'm very thankful of that fact because he shared so many things with grandpa that he then passed on to me.

Ernest Hemingway oftentimes talked about the story. He was not greatly concerned about the length of the manuscript but the quality of the story. I have tried to keep that in mind as I wrote about Ezra's experiences. I did not add to or subtract from the book for any reasons. I was constantly aware of keeping the content to what I'd heard from my grandfather and keeping it historically accurate. The stories about fighting off the dogs, escaping through the tunnel, swimming across the Ohio River, and many other parts are the way I'd heard them from my grandfather "through the mouth of Ezra." There was some problem of knowing exactly where Ezra's small group was, since the state of West Virginia was brought into the Union in 1863. They were never quite sure during their escape whether they were in the Commonwealth of Virginia or had moved into the new state of West Virginia. Consequently, I had to do a little creative writing.

However, the clarity and truthfulness of the story has not been altered. Regardless of which state they were in, their experiences were the same. The overwhelming concern in the minds of these three men was to find the Ohio River and cross it.

Of course I never knew Ezra since he died many years before I was born, but through my grandfather, I gained the feeling that I did know him. This feeling became even stronger in me as I wrote this book. It was very easy for me to understand grandpa's stories about Ezra since I also am a US Army veteran. I always sensed from my grandfather that Ezra had a healthy respect for the Confederates he fought against. He saw them as young men who also fought for a cause they warmly embraced. I think in many ways that Ezra was a classic "salt-of-the-earth" type who simply left his home and farm to fight for patriotic reasons. He saw that conflict as a terrible but very necessary war.

I am very grateful to my grandfather for remembering so many things and sharing them with me. Without his help, this book could not have been accurately written. I am sure that many times I was a nuisance to him and love and respect him even more for tolerating my youth. Of course my thanks also go out to Ezra Hezekiah Van Buren, who made it possible for us to truly discover what those times were like.

James E. Ryhal

Springfield, Ohio

Chapter 1

The sun was hot and the weather warm for only the second week of April. In spite of the heat, it seemed like it rained every other week. If this weather with the heat and rain continued, the fields would yield a very large corn crop in August. I lay on the old swing on our front porch. The sun felt wonderful on my pants and slowly eased me into sleep. The air was cool, but the sun was very warm and penetrated my clothing. There was much work scheduled for me, but I preferred to think about sleep rather than work, regardless of how important it was.

My mother had finished her baking in the kitchen. Through the dining room and entire house, the aroma from the pies permeated the air. The aroma covered the first floor, rose to the second floor, and even moved out of the house onto the porch where I lay. She had baked two apple pies and two peach pies. The fruit from each pie came from our little backyard orchard. The heat and the aroma from the pies put me to sleep, and I began to dream. In my bedroom and on my dresser was a large blue glass jar where I collected coins. It was only half full, but by the end of the summer, it should be overflowing, and I planned to purchase a small Winchester rifle. I imagined my targets for my little Winchester. Raccoons, woodchucks, and even deer from time to time came into my little forest. There were dogs, mostly wild, that also came to our land, and they became targets for me. They molested our sheep and killed many lambs. Consequently, they became my favorite targets. My father had purchased two large goats that he left with our sheep, and they did not approve of any dogs being near our sheep and the lambs. The goats would drive the dogs away, but I would need my rifle for the feral dogs.

I remember the day very well: April 12, 1861. It became probably the most significant day in my life, but I did not realize that at the time. Years later we would remember that date. I remember this day — even the smallest detail in it. It would never be an easy day to forget.

Someone had come into my life and began to take part in my dream. Her name was Clarinda Jackson. I did not forget nor would I want to forget her precious smile. With her smile, I felt as if she had never smiled at anyone but me, and I'm sure she knew that. Her brown eyes and soft light hair were noticed by everyone. Her hair seemed to shine even when the sun was not upon it. Her tiny waist magnified her hips and her robust bosom made it impossible for me to look away. I wondered if other young men noticed these things in their sweethearts the way I constantly seemed to notice them. I concluded that they probably did, but nevertheless it was the way I felt, and I loved every moment of it.

"Ezra," came a familiar voice from inside the house. I could clearly hear the voice and knew it was my mother, but I didn't want to be awakened or to leave the comfortable porch swing. I never believed she would stop calling me, despite my silence, but I hoped she would.

"Ezra," came the voice the second time from the house. Again my mother called, but the sun would not permit me to answer. I continued to remain quiet, hoping she would give up and I could fall back into my pleasant dreams. The cold air was evaporating, and the sun now warmed me completely.

"Ezra Hezekiah Van Buren, where are you? I know you can hear me! Where are you?"

"I was sleeping here on the front porch. What is it you want?"

"I want you to come in here immediately! I have several important things to ask you."

I moved slowly into the room where she was. I could see by her serious demeanor that I should listen completely to her questions. "Did you repair those two loose boards next to the back porch door?" she asked.

"No, but I will as soon as we finish talking. I won't forget. Don't worry — I won't forget."

"Today was also the day that you were to help me plant lettuce and radishes in the garden."

"No, I forgot that also, but don't worry — I'll help you as soon as I'm through with these two little boards. Anything else?" I asked.

"Two more things," she said. "Your cousin has taken the wagon to Columbus and will be back tonight."

"When tonight?" I asked.

"After supper, probably pretty late, but that doesn't matter. He was planning to help you with the fence, but now you'll have to do it alone. You will also need to repair the pen that holds the lambs. I am afraid some of them will get loose if you don't do it today. You must do it before tonight. You should be able to do that — it's very important."

"Yes ma'am, I'll get it done. You said that you had two things to tell me. What's the other thing?"

She scratched her chin. "I can't remember," she said. "I just can't remember."

I started to the barn for a hammer and nails to repair the two boards on the back porch. "I remember now," she said. "I remember the last thing I wanted to ask you. Did you hear about the fighting?"

"What fighting?"

"The fighting in South Carolina," she said. "They fired on some fort near the ocean."

"What fort?" I asked.

"Fort Sumter."

"Who was it that fired on this fort?"

"Apparently some South Carolinians," she said. "I don't know whether they were civilians or the South Carolina National Guard. Your cousin will know more about that when he returns tonight from Columbus. He's undoubtedly heard a lot about it there, and he'll tell us. He'll tell you all about it, I'm sure. I'm sorry, son, I don't know many details."

"I honestly don't know what you're talking about, Mother. I'm sorry, I just can't figure out what is happening."

"Wait until tonight. Your cousin or your father will explain it. Wait 'til tonight."

"I wonder if it means a war," I said.

"Ask your cousin or father tonight."

"Fort Sumter," I said softly. "I'm certain I never heard of it before, never heard of it."

"Your father didn't seem very concerned about it when he left; therefore, I wouldn't worry too much," she said.

"Fort Sumter," I said again. "Fort Sumter."

*   *   *   *   *

My father and cousin returned home late at night and the next day had much news for us. Columbus, Ohio, was completely buzzing over the attack on Fort Sumter, and there was much talk of war. Several legislators had returned from Washington, but they were not greatly alarmed. The feeling in the nation's capital was that any conflict would be over in several weeks — several months at most. In Washington they were calling it the War of Rebellion, but in Columbus, our state capital, they were calling it the Coming War Between the States.

Some in Washington were trying to decide how to punish any seceding state, particularly South Carolina. Other legislators waited to see exactly how many states might leave the Union. Nearly everyone seemed to agree there would be an armed conflict. President Lincoln had begun to call for volunteers. My father and I did not discuss my enlistment, yet I felt certain that each of us knew the other was thinking greatly about it.

Strangely, some legislators in Washington talked of letting the southern states go and form their own federation. This subject greatly angered my father and me and made me realize that my own enlistment was probably inevitable. I had never heard any talk in central Ohio about letting southern states leave the Union, but apparently in Washington that talk was not uncommon.

Those in Columbus who had returned from the nation's capital had said there were many Southern congressmen still in Washington waiting to hear from their own states about if and when they should return home. These congressmen talked constantly of states' rights and rebellion. It was difficult to imagine we were actually talking about the breakup of our country. Feelings were running deeply, and the divisions between us were deeper than I realized.

Chapter 2

Our home was about twenty-five miles west of Upper Sandusky, Ohio, on U.S. Route 30, northwest of Columbus. We lived in Wyandot County on a farm of 280 acres, six miles north of Forest and approximately five miles south of Wharton. It was a well-traveled road that came out of Pennsylvania from the east and traveled to Indiana to the west.

Most of the timber was cut from the farm to gain farmland before I was born. Our family had come here from Albany County, New York, and the land had small plots of trees left on it similar to the forty acres in the northern part of our farm.

I always referred to these forty acres as "my forest." Of course these acres were not mine but part of the family farm. However, I walked in the north forty acres and seemed to appreciate them more than anyone else in the family, and for this reason, I considered them to be mine. From my earliest memories, I found pleasure just walking in them and, in my later years, hunting on them. I felt a peace in my forest that I experienced nowhere else. Walnut trees were the most numerous here, but there were many white oak, hickory, beech, and a few apple trees. There were raccoons and rabbits in my forest. After a few years, deer filtered into it and made their homes there. Large fox squirrels also lived there, and in the fall, I hunted them the most. These squirrels climbed to the very top of the large white oaks and were not an easy target for me. In April and May, the deer had their fawns there, and I deliberately stayed out of the forest during these months.

The war was on my mind now, and I didn't dwell upon it, but like everyone else, I couldn't put it completely out of my mind. Several friends from Wyandot County had already enlisted with the Union forces. I did not like the thought of raising my rifle and aiming at another man. And it was even more difficult to think of drawing a revolver at close range on another person. With a revolver, I would see my opponent's face very clearly and know exactly who I was killing.

Suddenly, and in complete silence, a huge dark bird landed in a great white oak only fifty feet from me. It was a great red-tailed hawk, and I sat totally motionless at the base of a small apple tree, watching the bird. I breathed slowly so even my breathing could not be heard. I knew the vision of this bird was great, and I never moved. The hawk turned its head to the left and then to the right, like a sentry. Although I never moved, I was certain he would discover who I was and what I was. My father had told me that only the wolf and the hawk could distinguish the human animal, even when they never move. I could see the thin tail of a field mouse hanging down from the hawk's talon.

Now he stood motionless and looked only at me. Not a muscle did I move; I did not even blink my eyes. No matter — he knew what I was and burst from the branch into the air with the mouse falling to the ground.

For what seemed like a long time, I sat motionless at the base of the apple tree, hoping he would return to recover his mouse. But he did not return and probably would never return for the little field mouse. He would undoubtedly catch other mice but wouldn't return now because he had seen the human creature, who he knew was his enemy. After probably forty minutes, I rose from the ground and went to the base of the white oak tree where he had perched. In the short wet grass, directly under his perch, I found the tiny gray mouse. I held it in my hand, fascinated by its smallness. The tiny eyes, ears and feet fit completely into the palm of my hand. It was the smallest creature I'd ever seen — and he lived in my forest.

My thoughts returned to the war. If I joined my friends and volunteered, I would not see Claire for perhaps a long time — I did not know how long. But the time I would be away probably wouldn't be that long. The fighting might be terrible for a short time, but everyone seemed to agree that it would be over in a few weeks, certainly within a few months. I could live without her for a short time. During that time, I'd also be with my friends, and they'd also be apart from loved ones. Whatever the length of time, it would not be long, and I could save my earnings during my enlistment. My small fears faded away, and I thought I'd probably even return before the fall harvest. Let the Rebels worry about the struggle — I would not. Everyone knew the Rebels started the rebellion, and we should let them grieve over its length. I'd be home with Claire in a short while.

Tomorrow after Sunday worship there would be a church dinner, and I'd see her then. I had no more thoughts of the war — only of her. A pleasant feeling came over me, but that feeling always came over me when I thought about her. No more thoughts of the conflict — only her. A tiny smile came to my face, and it came because of my thoughts of her.

Chapter 3

The sanctuary of the Wharton Methodist Church was full that Sunday — actually it was overfilled, and ushers brought chairs to the rear of the room. The church windows were open, and a cool breeze circulated over the pews. The church was never this filled, except at the Christmas season and usually during Holy Week at Easter.

I moved slowly to an empty space on a pew that was directly in the center of the sanctuary. This morning even the balcony was filling with the faithful. I watched the worshippers from below, and there she was in the balcony – my Clarinda. Her family was with her, but none of them noticed me or even looked down to the pews below. I watched her for about a minute, and I could feel a tiny smile come to my face.

I eased myself onto the new oak pew and now looked to the front of the church, toward the pulpit and communion table. I was tempted to turn toward the balcony and look at her again, but I did not. My pride kept me from turning, and it would be very obvious that I was continuing to look back and up toward her. We sang the opening hymn that everyone knew, and because the attendance was so large and the windows were open, our voices resonated probably a mile from our country church.

The pastor's sermon was powerful and, thankfully, not too long. He showed a certain presence that I hadn't seen before. His words were uplifting and spoke to our divided country and God's plan for us. The large attendance was undoubtedly due to the church dinner and the anxiety of a possible coming war and not simply because of his message. Nevertheless, I was glad I was there that morning.

Most of the congregation meandered slowly from the sanctuary to the eighteen tables on the west side of the church. Others went to the basement to bring food outside to the tables. Outside, I waited for my mother and our family, as well as Claire and the Jackson family. When everyone had arrived outside, our pastor returned thanks.

Farm families knew how to prepare fine food and, with few exceptions, loved to eat it. Roast beef, hams, cheeses, and bread were everywhere. Two long tables held corn, beans of all kinds, fruits, and drinks. But the jewel of all the tables was the dessert table holding cakes and pies. Pies made from apples, peaches, blueberries, and cherries were abundant and were wonderful.

At the opposite end of the table, Claire smiled at me and my family. It seemed natural that people began to speak of the war. Everyone felt certain it would be a short conflict and would happily end soon. For some reason, I didn't wish to talk about the conflict and didn't enter into the conversation. I concentrated on Claire and my cherry pie. After finishing the pie, I concentrated only on her.

The two of us left the table and walked away from the crowd. I held her hand, and we walked a long distance. The grass on the lawn, the cornfield next to us, and the leaves on the trees were green and seemed endless. They had a wonderful fragrance as we walked a long way from the church building and never spoke.

Our silence was more important than anything else to us. Although nothing was said, we knew there would never be anyone else for either of us. We stopped at a freshly planted cornfield. The sprouts of green corn were only three or four inches high.

We turned and looked back at the path we had come from and could see the church. We could see others at the tables, but the distance was too far for us to see their faces. We were alone in our own world now.

"I worry that you'll forget me and things will be different," she said.

"Things will not be different," I said. "Nothing is going to change us."

"Are you certain you will love me at least a little when you're gone?"

"I'll have to think about that," I said.

"What is it you have to think about?"

"About loving you a little. No, I don't think I'll love you a little. I can only love you a lot."

I let go of her hand and put my arms around her and kissed her a long time. I kissed her a second time, and she put her arms around me also. One more time, I wanted to kiss her and crush her bosom against me, but she stopped me.

"That's enough, Ezra, besides we should start back," she said. "They will be missing us."

Holding her hand again, we began to retrace our steps back to the church dinner. "Did you hear there were two more boys from Wyandot County that enlisted?" she asked.

"No! I did not know that. Where were they from? Do I know them?"

"They lived in Forest, just south of Route 30, toward Upper Sandusky," she said.

"What were their names," I asked.

"They were the Martin boys, Billie and Charlie. I think that you knew Billie."

"Oh yes, I knew him. He was in my class at school, and I graduated with him."

"Did you know his brother?" she asked.

"No, I did not know him. He was a few years older than we were. I might've seen him once or twice, but I never knew him. And did you say they enlisted together?"

"Yes, they did."

"That's rather amazing," I said. "I hope they get to serve in the same unit together."

"I hope so, too. They probably will," she said.

"I didn't even know there was an enlistment office around here," I said.

"There isn't one around here," she replied. "They went to Huron County to enlist."

"Are you certain? I never heard of any army post in Huron County."

"They enlisted in the 123rd Ohio Infantry at Camp Monroeville in Huron County. They enlisted for three years," she said softly.

"Three years," I said. "It seems like a very long time — three years. Wow!"

"I don't think that really matters," Claire said.

"What do you mean, it doesn't matter? Three years is a long time! Three years away from your family, your sweetheart or your wife. The army tells you where you'll be and what you'll do for three years!"

"Everyone is certain the war will be over in a short time — probably a few weeks," she said. "At the very most, it will take only a few months."

She's probably right, I thought. It will probably be over in two or three months. That's why so many are enlisting. They're certain they'll be home in a short time — probably for the fall harvest.

I felt that I didn't have to worry about someone else coming into her life. After today, we would be together. Regardless of my time in the army, I knew she would wait for me. I knew.

Chapter 4

The 123rd Ohio Infantry left Huron County on October 16, 1862, for Parkersburg. By now I was a first lieutenant leading a fifty-man platoon. Strangely enough I looked forward to a struggle. We thought the quicker the fighting began, the quicker the Rebs would seek a truce. None of us believed the fighting would last long. I was twenty now and wanted this rebellion over, wishing to return to my other life. Every man in my platoon had that same feeling.

At New Creek, we saw our first action. The platoon worked a reconnaissance duty, and not a single man fired his rifle. In December we moved to Petersburg, and the fighting really began. The Confederates could shoot well and surprised us. This group obviously had more experience than we had, but we gave back as much as we received that day. For the first time, I saw a man in a gray suit fall from my rifle. I was not proud of my deed, but federal troops were falling around me, and all of us were loading our rifles as fast as possible and firing back. We were learning quickly.

We hid near a small creek, and the banks of it gave us cover as we licked our wounds. The tiny creek was a good place to hide. Although we did not advance, we kept the Rebels away.

I spread out the men in the platoon, and after several hours, the word came down from Colonel Wilson that we were to pull back to a better position. We were not happy with this order but realized it probably was some sort of strategic withdrawal.

Suddenly rifle fire was very heavy again, falling all around us. The Rebels would fire at us and then simply evaporate into the small forest, then show themselves and fire at us again. They had learned this trick somewhere, and our men had not quite figured it out. We waited for them to show themselves again, but they did not. We began to rest and clean some of our equipment. Suddenly they began to fire again. We realized they were alternating the different times that they showed themselves. Several men were wounded and one killed as we dug in deeper into our trenches. We were learning.

The fire had been heavy, yet we had survived our first struggle. Our men had fought well, and we had controlled our fear. We gave the Rebels their due, and they had fought well. Nevertheless, we remembered they were the enemy.

Chapter 5

It was called the Second Battle of Winchester. Our unit had not participated in the first battle but saw a bellyful of fighting in the second battle. The Rebels were better fighters than we were led to believe. They hid better than our men, and when they came out of hiding, they shot more quickly and accurately than our units.

Despite all the shooting and all the noise, we were not afraid. The men in our company fought bravely and gave no ground. It was probably our youth and our naiveté that gave us the strong feeling that we were invincible. Somehow we felt as twenty-year-olds that it would be someone else that would fall in battle. We certainly would never feel the pain of the musket ball tearing into us. Most of us felt we would live to be one hundred. But on this day, we learned that some of us would not make it to that age. We learned that we were not unconquerable. Some of us would not make it to age twenty-one.

Quickly there was a great increase in a terrible and viscous noise. Artillery shells burst all around us, and we scrambled for anything that gave us cover and protection. I lay behind a large tree trunk with several others in the company. The bursting of shells slowly moved away from us, and we realized the shells were from Union guns on Confederate lines as they also retreated. I rose from the ground and led the company of troops after the Rebels. We charged steadily but not recklessly. The bursting of shells from our cannons continued to move away from us and kept striking the Rebel lines. Small-arms fire whizzed past my head, and instinctively I fell to the ground.

"Down, men," I yelled. Somehow the Rebels had now gotten our range. "Stay down until I give the order!"

It was now obvious to me that the gray uniforms were gone — nowhere in view. Where they would make a stand, we did not know, but we felt certain they would simply not leave the battlefield to us.

The battalion surgeon had the men moved back to a hospital area, and we waited. The Rebels very clearly were managing the fight to suit their own strategy, and we had not learned how to counter the action.

My first sergeant came to me and asked, "Lieutenant, is there any way we can call in artillery on their position? We can't get at them because they have better defensive positions than we have."

He was right.

"Take two men, Sergeant, and find the battalion artillery. Tell them what we need and be certain none of the shells fall on our position. After the bombardment, we can make plans to attack their positions or outflank them. Now pick your two men and get moving immediately."

I picked four of our best snipers and showed them the last position where we had seen the Rebels. They were to cover that position and look for the Rebs when they popped up and shot at us again. The artillery barrage passed over our lines and was now landing in the last position where we had seen the Confederates. Trees were struck and split in half as the bombardment continued. Huge holes in the ground were made as the shells hit. The Rebels returned no fire at us, and we began to wonder if they were still there. A strange quietness came over our battlefield, and no shots rang out after the artillery barrage stopped.

I sent out a patrol to see if they could find the enemy's position. For a good period of time, we waited and heard no gunfire. For the better part of an hour, we waited for our patrol to return or the enemy to fire upon us. One of our men returned, and a few minutes later, the others came also. They found nothing and learned that the Confederates had withdrawn.

I was disturbed the way the enemy could withdraw from us so silently without us even getting a few shots at them. I was certain this was a veteran group of Rebels that we'd encountered. Their marksmanship and their deception in the woods convinced me they'd been in many battles before. We were tempted to pursue them, but since the patrol had not seen them, we had no idea where they were, and I was afraid of walking into an ambush.

My platoon was scattered, and I sent out five men to bring them back together. After a short while, they returned, and we were now complete.

My first sergeant said, "Thank God we have no casualties, Lieutenant. I don't think anyone even got a scratch."

We began to dig in our foxholes and our trenches. We were not exactly certain where the Rebels were, but knew we were safer in the ground. I called to our command post and two experienced sergeants to find the battalion headquarters. Before we moved any further, we needed to know what orders we had or to simply stay put.

"Lieutenant, exactly where is battalion headquarters? Which direction should we head — I need to know."

"I don't know, Sergeant! I feel certain it's somewhere behind us. The Rebels took off in the opposite direction in front of us, so you'll just have to ask any of our troops you encounter behind us."

"Sir, what do we ask them at battalion?"

"Everything you can think of. Do we stay here for the night? Do we go out on patrol and look for the enemy? Do we leave early in the morning for another attack? Ask them everything that is important and try to be back here before dark."

"Yes, sir," they answered, as they quickly disappeared into the forest.

Almost three hours later, they returned and gave us the battalion orders that we were to bivouac here for the rest of the night. Ninety minutes after sunrise, the battalion is to move westward. The cavalry will lead out all forces, and we are to follow them.

It was a good order, I thought. The men were beat, and all of us needed rest. Skies were clear that night, and millions of stars told us there would be no rain. The grass was very thick and felt like a heavily feathered bed. If we had to sleep in the open, this was a perfect place.

I put out sentries, and everyone slept well. I only hoped the sentries would keep awake. I spread my blankets on the thick grass and settled in. We would have no trouble sleeping tonight — every man in the platoon was very tired. I closed my eyes and dreamt of Clarinda, only Clarinda.

The next morning, we learned the Rebels had moved out quietly during the night. They did a good job in their retreat; we never heard them, and their wagons and horses seemed invisible.

* * * * *

The new year had begun, and in January, we moved to Romney. For a while, we were held in reserve but knew that we would see fighting very soon. We were strangely anxious to fight. We seemed to have a taste for battle after our last fighting and were very confident. We were no longer in awe of the Confederates and began to feel we were better troops.

The weather was terrible, and the rain never stopped. Some of us began to feel that the heavy rain was a bad omen, but we pushed it out of our minds. It rained hard and steady for two days. Clouds constantly moved and kept the sun from touching us. The days were very dreary and began to grow cold. Our raincoats failed us, and everyone wore soaked clothing.

The fighting began again, and the rifle fire was continuous. Thank God the fighting helped us to ignore the rain, but slowly all of us began to shake from body chills. We knew the outdoor temperature was dropping, and there was nowhere to find warmth. A corporal came to me from our right flank and reported on the fighting.

"Sir, there's a large group of the enemy to our right, and they appear to be trying to outflank us," he said.

"That can't be accurate, Corporal. We've had no reports on enemy activity except those directly in front of us."

"Sir, we're taking fire on our right flank and are falling from rifle fire from the enemy."

"Corporal, I can't move any troops in your direction without more confirmation than simply one man."

"Lieutenant, I can bring someone from my squad, and they will tell you the same thing. Almost all of them have been hit."

"How badly have they been hit?"

"Some are dead or dying. The fire is withering. They blindsided us, and many were killed before we knew where they were."

"Lieutenant Van Buren," shouted a young man who came running to us.

"I am Lieutenant Van Buren. What is it you want, soldier? Corporal, do you know this man?"

"Yes, he is in my squad. He will confirm that the Rebels have turned the corner and are now behind us. We are receiving fire from three sides. If we don't move to our left, they're obviously going to surround us."

"God have mercy! Pass the word down the line that everyone is to turn on the left flank and try to break out. We'll set a new defense line as soon as we've moved. Get moving!"

We began to move but slowly. Some of the troops had wounds and were heavy-laden with their soaked uniforms. We passed the word, but the left-flank maneuver was becoming a nightmare in slow motion. Some men simply ran to the left away from the fighting, oftentimes without their weapons. Other men dug in and hid behind downed trees or rocks for cover, even though they were ordered to move. If half our forces escaped encirclement, it would be a miracle. The desire to dig in and fire back at the Rebels was strong. We wanted to strike back at this enemy who had attacked us, yet at the same time we knew we must move and escape encirclement.

As we ran, we made moving targets of ourselves but could not help it if we wanted to escape. I urged them on, and most of them continued to run and shoot at the same time. Our marksmanship was very poor. We had to stop and reload and then become targets ourselves. Occasionally we saw a gray figure fall as we fired, but more blue uniforms lay on the ground around us. In desperation, we stopped.

Suddenly it became almost quiet. We dropped down for cover and used logs and tree trunks to steady our rifles. A few shots were fired, and then there was silence — complete silence. We wondered what it meant.

After about fifteen minutes, we saw a blue uniform walking briskly toward us. I recognized him. It was Sergeant Greene. We saluted.

"Sir," said the sergeant, "there's a Rebel captain with a private carrying a white flag who wishes to talk to an officer."

"Sergeant, there are a dozen Union officers who outrank me who should be seeing this captain."

"Most are dead or wounded, sir."

"You must be crazy!"

"No sir — not crazy at all; we've checked everywhere. Many are dead and several badly wounded."

"I can't believe this!"

"Lieutenant, that Rebel captain has been waiting. We should see him very soon or he may leave."

"A white flag, you say?"

"Yes sir. You don't suppose he's surrendering to us? They couldn't be surrendering after the beating we've just taken."

"I wouldn't think so," I said. "All right, Sergeant. Let's go see what he wants before he thinks we're not coming."

We followed the tracks in the mud that the sergeant had made toward the Confederate lines. I tried not to look at the dead or wounded in either colored uniforms. Many had died horribly.

In the distance, we could see the Rebel captain and his sergeant with the white flag. We saluted each other.

"What does your white flag mean?"

"It does not indicate surrender, sir. It's meant to please hold your fire while we advance to meet your commander."

"What is it you wish?"

"My colonel wishes me to inform you that all federal forces are surrounded. You have many dead and even more wounded."

"What is your message?"

"Lieutenant, your troops have fought well, but your position in this forest is hopeless. My colonel urges you, in the name of humanity, to surrender. There is no need for more bloodshed. You will be well-treated. You must surrender. You are surrounded."

We stood there silently. I knew why he had come and what he was about to say before he even spoke. I bit my tongue firmly to keep back the tears. I nodded affirmatively, but I did not speak. Slowly he turned from us and returned to his lines.

We stacked our rifles, surrendered our revolvers and started the march eastward to Virginia and Libby Prison. It was a long and bitter march — cold and raining — a march we would not quickly forget.

Chapter 6

For nearly five hours, we marched eastward carrying our wounded. The Confederates promised to bury our dead using their chaplains, but we never knew exactly where. We paused for short rests and tried to dry ourselves with little success.

In front of us, the city of Richmond appeared, and we saw the James River. At last, and totally exhausted, we saw the prison building. Libby Prison was a four-story plain brick building with no distinguishing features. Its dismal look was only broken by some white paint. On the outside, the first two levels were painted white and the top two floors were left in their original dark red brick. It had four chimneys and was located on the old Tobacco Road.

No one was ever released from Libby — a few escaped, and many died. Approximately a dozen men died each night. The Rebels wouldn't even come inside the prison to remove the dead. If a man died in a bunk next to you, the Union prisoner on each side of him took his body to the first floor to be removed by the Confederates and buried.

Some men died from wounds, others from infections. Overcrowding was very bad, but most men died from lack of hope. Everyone hoped for escape or an end to the war. Everyone hoped to be with their families and on their homesteads again. I hoped for Claire and to embrace her again.

Hope is a good thing. It was the only thing we had, and it kept most of us alive. I reread 1 Corinthians 13 in the New Testament. I had read it many times previously but never had really understood it until now. St. Paul understood hope, and he helped me and my comrades.

The prison had eight large rooms and actually opened in 1861. Because of the high death toll, Libby was generally regarded as second only to Andersonville in its depravity. Libby Prison held only Union officers. We never knew exactly where our enlisted men were sent. The Rebels had separated our group between officers and enlisted men shortly before we reached Richmond. We never saw the others again.

We settled into our uneasy new life, and boredom quickly arrived for all of us. After only a few weeks, plans for escape began to crop up. Our feelings about a short war began to fade. We had no idea how long the war would continue and we would be at Libby, but the days turned into weeks and the weeks turned into months. There was much talk about prisoner exchanges, and we hoped the talk was true.

The Confederates permitted some letter writing, but it was greatly limited. Letters were limited to only families at our home and to six lines in each letter. Most men asked their families to send them cornstarch, pickles, sausages, and mostly socks. Money was never requested because it never would arrive.

No one wrote about prison exchanges after a few months. President Lincoln had stopped the exchanges because the Rebels were helped more by this than our forces. There was bitterness toward Lincoln about the stoppage of exchanges, but we simply had to put it out of our minds.

Keeping warm at Libby was difficult for us. One blanket was not enough to keep us warm, for the northern part of Virginia had snow, like Ohio. As the weather grew warmer, a few of us were permitted outside the building to work. Those who were permitted to work outside tried to bring back vegetables and fruits. They brought in onions, peppers, carrots, apples, peaches and wild strawberries. Anything that was scrounged up for us was a great treat. Sometimes we got a real feast of sweet potatoes. One day a young prisoner brought back a dead rabbit. It seemed as if it had been secretly killed, so no one wanted to eat it. Protein was something we greatly needed, and we decided to cut the rabbit into pieces and thoroughly roast it.

Looting and thievery were common, so we guarded our valuables closely. There was little money, so most things were bartered. Guards did a thriving business, and corn whiskey was used as a common currency. Knives, watches, scissors, needles, buttons, and clothing were very difficult to have in the South, so the guards particularly looked for these. Common items were greatly in demand by the guards, and we could follow the course of the war by the items needed by the Confederacy.

Of course a trader of goods could get into trouble. As the war continued, guards and prisoners each grew more careful. Despite the degradation of looting and bartering, many men showed charity and rediscovered their Christian duty. A few men regularly read the Bible to those who were obviously dying. Some of our men stared into space, and they usually were gone by morning.

Early one morning, I helped a friend carry a body to the first floor. We paused to catch our breath and heard two Rebel guards talking.

"We sure as hell must've underestimated these damned Yankees," said a tall Confederate sergeant.

"How do you figure that?" asked his friend.

"This is the third year of this war, and they ain't showed no signs of quittin'. They jest keep a fightin'. I figured they'd be quittin' before this. Our officers told us they had no stomach for fightin'."

"I reckon they were wrong, Sergeant, you're right about that."

After this I ate and returned to my bunk. The sun was out from the clouds, and I would've preferred to be outside, but I had no working pass, so I lay on my bunk and rested.

"Ezra," someone said. "Ezra," someone said again.

My eyes stayed closed, but I said, "Who is it, and what do you want?"

"It's Lieutenant Charles Redman, and I need you to come to my bunk. It's important."

I really didn't want to leave my bunk; it was warm, and I needed the rest. I felt if I stayed quiet, Redman might leave and forget to talk to me. I began to drift into sleep. For what seemed to be the better part of an hour, I dozed.

"Ezra, I thought you were coming to my bunk," Redman said.

He had not forgotten me, and at last I opened my eyes. I rose from my bunk and slowly walked to his bunk at the other side of the room.

"Ezra, I got two things I want to tell you," Redman said.

"What are they? They must not be very important," I said.

"Yes they are," he said. "One is important and one is very important."

"Tell me the one that's important first."

"Do you know our regimental doctor? His name is Perry, Captain Perry — tall, slender guy."

"I don't know him, but I know who he is. But what about him?"

"His wife sent him a shirt, a brand-new, blue, long-sleeved shirt."

"How do you know that?" I asked.

"I saw the damned thing."

"And it got past the Rebel censor?"

"Yes."

"You're either joking or lying. Some Rebel guard would surely have stolen that thing."

"I saw it, and it looked beautiful. It will help keep him warm this winter. I wish to hell I had one coming for myself," he said.

"That's really hard to believe, but if you saw it, then I guess it's true."

"I saw it," he repeated.

"I believe you. I believe you. Now what is the very important news? Don't tell me someone else has gotten new clothing."

"No, I'm not telling you that. This is much bigger than that." He paused and motioned with his finger for me to come closer to him.

"What is it?" I whispered.

"There's a strong rumor floating around that the Confederates are moving this camp to Georgia, either Macon or Andersonville."

"You're crazy! That's too far to move any camp. When is this supposed to happen?"

"Not right away, but it's more than a strong rumor. In fact, one of our people has confirmed it. I don't know when it's to take place, but it's true. In fact, we've already formed an escape committee, and they want you on it."

"How are they going to do this?"

"Tunnel. Tunnel," he said. "They've even started digging. It's pretty small, but at least they've begun."

"Already?"

"Hell, it's going to take a while," he said. "If we start digging now, we've got to finish that tunnel before we're scheduled to go to Georgia. We simply can't wait. It's got to be done in a short time. We can't wait for anything. We surely don't want to go to Georgia."

"You're right," I said. "I wasn't thinking about the time to dig it. Will you be going with us?"

"You can bet on that! How about yourself?"

"Hell, yes," I said. "I'm on the committee. Remember?"

Chapter 7

The Rebs had armed guards all around Libby Prison. If a Union soldier was standing near a window, he could be, and oftentimes was, shot. He didn't have to be doing anything — he was simply a target. We learned very quickly to keep back in the shadows, away from any window. The practice had little to do with security. Most windows were twenty to thirty feet from the ground. Many ankles and legs were broken in jumps for freedom, and the jumping quickly stopped. Even if a successful jump was made, the Rebel guards quickly shot the escapee. Prisoners learned it was simply hatefulness that caused the guards to shoot since prisoners had long stopped jumping.

Libby had some unusual peculiarities. Sunday was different. Six days a week the guards shot those near the windows at Libby but not on the Sabbath.

The Confederates permitted chapel services, and guards stopped their deadly fun. Two Union chaplains held services, one on the second floor and one on the third floor of the brick prison.

We celebrated the Lord's Supper this Sunday, and I stood in the back of the room waiting to come forward. Wes was with me that Sunday. His name was John Wesley Williams, but everyone called him Wes.

"Ezra, did you see the guy over there to our right?" Wes asked.

"You mean the tall skinny kid?"

"That's the one," Wes said. "He's so skinny. I'm sure he's only eighteen, but he looks about eighty."

"What's wrong with his mouth?" I asked.

"Can't you tell? He's got scurvy. Can't you notice how his teeth look loose, like they're falling out?"

"God have mercy," I said. "He's probably not twenty years old, and he looks like he's a hundred. You talk like you know him."

"We enlisted together at the same time, but this is the first time I've seen him since that day. After we celebrate communion, I want to walk over and see him. Will you go over with me?"

"Certainly," I said. The line moved forward for the sacrament, but it moved slowly. Our chaplain consecrated the elements of bread and wine, and we passed steadily in the long line.

"There's your friend," I said to Wes.

"Where?"

"Near that far wall, standing by himself."

Wes approached him and spoke. "Didn't you enlist when I did in Ohio? You look familiar."

The young man smiled. "I think so," he said. "We were later captured at High Bridge and then sent here to Libby."

"I too was captured at High Bridge," Wes said.

"We were all captured at High Bridge," I said. "All the officers at that battle were sent here — even the chaplains."

As we talked, I couldn't help notice his long pants. Despite his thinness, his trousers bulged below his waist on his right leg.

"What's wrong with your belt and waistband on those trousers?" I asked.

"Nothing," said the young man.

"Let me see that," I said as I reached for his belt. I could feel that it was very hard and clearly was a revolver.

"Don't touch that," he said.

"What is that?" Wes said.

"He's got a damn revolver hidden under his waistband."

"I don't," he said.

"The hell you don't! That's why you didn't want me to touch your belt or waistband," I said.

"You're crazy!"

"Don't give me that crap," I snarled. "You're skinny as a rail. If I can see that revolver, you know damn well one of these Rebel guards can see it too."

For probably the first time in the war, I was very frightened. The young fool had no idea the danger he'd brought to all of us. At the first sight of a hidden revolver, the Rebs could start shooting from every direction.

"Ezra, I think you should let him keep it," Wes said. "After all, it belongs to him."

"Wes, keep out of this!"

"But Ezra…"

"Wes, shut up! Both of you, shut up! If they find that handgun, they can legally kill everyone in this prison. They can claim the revolver constitutes an armed rebellion or attempt to break out. Neither of you knows what this means," I said.

"Then what should we do?" Wes asked.

"We've got to get it out of this building," I said. "We can drop it in the trench at the latrine."

"If you guys had any idea how difficult it was to get that revolver in here, you wouldn't ask me to give it up, but I'll give it to you. I don't want anyone getting in any more trouble," said our skinny friend. Finally he seemed to understand.

* * * * *

The sun was down now, and it was very dark. It was so dark, I couldn't see the horizon. The darkness was good, for no sentry could now see me. The only problem was that it would affect my vision, and I must be very careful. I could fall over anything — even into the latrine. For a long time, I stood in the doorway while my eyes adjusted to the darkness. Only the crickets were my companions. Unlike many prisons, Libby had no guards inside the brick building. In daylight hours, the sentry gave a prisoner permission to go to the latrine. In the darkness, a Rebel may ignore a prisoner near the latrine or shoot him — whatever the sentry's discretion. I was in a bad position, and for a moment, I wished I'd let the kid keep the damned revolver. Yet if he kept it, he surely would've been caught. If I tried to hide it somewhere in the building, an inspecting guard would've found it sooner or later. Now I could be caught hiding in the darkness heading to the latrine. If I threw it in the latrine, I could even be shot returning to the building. I was in a hell of a mess. Like a giant spider web, there was danger in whatever I did. I moved very slowly.

I stepped through the doorway and strangely began to gain some confidence. The blackness was more of a help than a hindrance. I found some trees on my path and stood beside them before I moved. I could now smell the latrine and moved toward the odor. After disposing of the revolver, I would get away from the latrine as quickly as possible.

From time to time, the moon came out from behind the clouds and gave some light to help me. My clothing was dark, and I stood still when the moon was out and moved silently only when it returned behind the cloud. I was in no hurry. Speed was not part of my plan.

At last I reached the latrine. I resisted an overwhelming desire to throw the gun. I realized that much movement might be noticed, and I could also even miss the trench. From only a few feet away, I lowered the pistol into the foul water. Now I had to find the same route to return to the prison. I grew a little anxious and walked more quickly. Then I stopped. I was not alone.

I could see movement to my left and stayed behind a tree. It was probably a Confederate guard but also possibly a Union officer, like myself. I would never know.

When I reached the barracks, I knew I was safe. I moved very quietly to the second floor. All the bunks were eighteen inches apart, and the smell of perspiration and body odor was strong. Most men snored, and it covered the small noise I made. I slipped under my blanket and thanked God for helping me.

Chapter 8

Life at Libby was tedious and very boring. Each day seemed longer than the previous one. I am certain that many Union prisoners died of monotony. They went to sleep and simply did not wake up. I did not try to fool myself; I knew I would also fall to the slow-moving and meaningless life. My long-term plan was escape, but I was not quite ready for that.

Consequently, I developed a new plan, almost a game, to help me. Mentally I would think of Claire in every way and place. I took less and less time to fall asleep at lights out. My mind got so efficient that other prisoners noticed how quickly I dozed off each night.

I closed my eyes and pictured her in different dresses that I remembered. I pictured her singing at church and even her dresses at church suppers. I pictured her brown eyes and light brown hair. I thought of her smile, her pretty hands, and her bosom. I pictured the winter at home, and I saw a red fox running across the snow toward the woods. On that bright snow, the fox looked like an orange ball, so light on its feet that it didn't break the upper crust of the snow but glided across it.

Every year Claire's father cut a huge Scotch pine from their farm and decorated it for a beautiful Christmas tree. I remembered these things well, and on certain nights, it seemed as though I could smell my mother cooking Thanksgiving turkey and pumpkin pie. In Claire's home, I could smell many cakes baked at Christmas. I thought of the day I would be home and hold her tightly. My favorite dream was one that was after we wed. My mind had become a powerful ally that helped me through many terrible days.

One terrible morning, I awoke and found the man next to me was dead. His name was Woodrow, but I never really knew him. I said a short prayer for him, and some Rebel guards came and told us to remove his body. In less than an hour, he was buried in the earth. There was really nothing special about his death — at least a dozen others died every night at Libby. Several days later, I noticed the markers placed in Union Cemetery and knew I must make serious plans for my future escape or I, too, would be in the same cemetery.

More and more prisoners arrived, and after the Battle of Chickamauga, 200 badly wounded prisoners arrived at Libby. Most were famished and starving. They told us they were three days on the road and had nothing to eat except four hard crackers. Many of these wounded lay two days before their wounds were dressed.

At Libby self-respect quickly vanished. Men were half-clad and covered with vermin. They were quickly beyond medical help. It seemed impossible that so much filth could be on dying men, but it was true. One day the ambulances brought eighteen men, and eleven had died by the next morning. I watched the ambulances closely and became even more convinced that I must move up the date of our escape.

Libby was taking in captured Union troops by the dozen but let no men out. The prisoners were huddled up and jammed into every corner and crook — at the bathing troughs and the round cooking stoves. Everywhere prisoners were jostling back and forth. Most men were too tired and weak from starvation to complain.

The prison had no windows — just heavy bars because a few men had injured themselves jumping to the ground. They took the severely injured ones away, and we never saw them again. The iron bars were called The Dead Line at Libby. Some did not know you couldn't lean out of the bars and were shot. Others learned fast; we stayed back.

Actually the countryside at Libby was beautiful, but none of us noticed it anymore. Around the building, the grass was worn down, and guards often stood with rifles and hostile bayonets. I thought more and more of escape. Strangely, I had never feared being killed in battle but began now to think about my own death more and more. The fear of starving and disease haunted me. Talk of escape was everywhere.

The war continued in all its nastiness, but I didn't think of it anymore. Despite the wounded men that continued to come to Libby, in my mind I moved further and further away from them and closer to Clarinda. I dreamt of how it would be with her when all this had passed. I pictured her face and the flowered dress she wore at our last church supper. I did anything that helped me think of her and take me away from Libby.

Other officers talked about their wives and sweethearts, and it easily helped me think of Claire in the same way. Nights were the hardest. The blacker the nights, the more loneliness they produced. I tried to keep away from my cot until I was very, very tired. The later I went to my bed, the more soundly I slept and the longer I slept 'til the bugle was blown.

Chapter 9

After learning of the tunnel, I could think of only two things — Claire and escape. I realized I must never make the trip to Georgia. If I made the trip south, I would surely die. Even if I managed to escape from that prison, I would have to travel nearly a thousand miles north through the entire Confederacy until I reached the Ohio River. I had no illusions. If a local sheriff or a member of any constabulary didn't get me, then a Rebel soldier or local farmer would ask me for identification and probably shoot me. If our group wasn't shot, we would probably starve from such a long journey. I grew very depressed just thinking about the long trek.

Now I put all my plans together to leave Libby. I calculated that if I went west and then north, it should be about 150 miles to the River. Most men would surely travel north or northwest after their escape. The Rebs would pursue them in those directions with most of their troops. Going due west would be safer. There was no way I could know for certain how many would break out, but at least a hundred would try. I wanted to keep away from this body of our troops, as most of them would probably go due north.

I spent my time almost exclusively in the tunnel. Strangely, the work uplifted me, and I thought only of our freedom — mine included. Keeping clean was difficult, but it was a must. If the Rebs noticed the fresh dirt on us, they would easily guess about our escape tunnel.

Charles Redman and John Wesley Williams worked with me in the tunnel, and I planned to ask them to be with me when we escaped. I liked them and knew they would keep quiet about our break. Going it alone was dangerous and would be very hard. You have to have a stomach for loneliness, and getting lost was always a possibility and could be deadly. A week before the break, I began to hide food and approach my friends. But in an act that greatly surprised me, my two friends came to me and urged me to join them. Three was a good number — small, yet big enough to give help and support to each other. A larger group would begin to attract attention.

Without realizing it, I was becoming somewhat of a hermit. At night I dreamed of Claire and my escape to the River. During the day, I tried to exhaust myself in the tunnel. This caused me to sleep better at night because I was always in a state of mild exhaustion. The leaders in the escape plan asked me not to work each day but to pace myself and be seen in the prison building. Reluctantly I agreed. I realized it was good strategy, and I wanted to do nothing that would tip off the Confederates. I wasn't any more noticeable than anyone else, but I was paranoid that I was being watched.

The revolver I had thrown into the latrine came into my mind. Of course there was no way of retrieving it now, but it came to my mind often. In much secrecy, I continued to hoard food. I didn't want anyone to think I was in the escape committee, but most men in their own way were planning the same thing. I realized that if I was not careful, my own comrades may be pilfering food from me.

One particular night, I was very tired from a long day in the tunnel and went to sleep almost immediately. Claire came into my dream, and although the dream was not clear, it seemed to be our wedding. She was dressed in white, and friends and family were with her. The next day, some of my comrades told me I was talking in my sleep. Of course I didn't remember anything but realized I must be very careful. I didn't want to reveal anything with the escape date growing nearer and nearer.

Early that morning, I was cold — very cold. I pulled the well-worn wool blanket up over my shoulders. Outside a cold, hard rain fell. In a short time, the rain appeared as if it would turn to snow, but it did not. If the temperature had dropped two or three more degrees, we would've had large white flakes. It was the first week in March, and a freakish drop in the temperature created a terrible cold. We all hoped the dreadful rain would stop as quickly as it had begun.

The following day, the skies cleared, and the rain stopped, but the cold stayed with us. We did not resume our work in the tunnel for three days, but when we resumed our digging, many other men came to dig — the word of escape was getting around to many prisoners.

Although we had no idea when the Confederates planned to move the camp to Georgia, we grew fearful. A controlled panic gripped us for several days. We knew we had to complete our work before any evacuation to Macon or Andersonville. As the temperature rose and warmed us, our spirits rose, and we resumed our digging.

As I was leaving the tunnel, I realized for the first time that I was suffering from claustrophobia and was breathing heavily. I slowed my walk, but my heavy breathing continued. From behind me, I heard a voice.

"Ezra, are you all right?"

I did not stop.

"Ezra, Ezra, are you all right?"

This time I stopped but did not turn around. Someone put a hand on my shoulder, but I did not turn around.

"Ezra, it's me, Redman, is there anything the matter?"

This time I turned, but my heavy breathing continued. He knew something was wrong. I decided not to hide my fears — they could see them anyway.

"I'm feeling trapped. What the hell will I do if I get hit with this halfway through the tunnel?"

"Ezra, do you know how long they are estimating it will take each man to get completely out of the tunnel?"

"No."

"A man will be out of the tunnel in about one minute. One minute — that's sixty seconds. Hell, a man can endure almost anything for sixty seconds."

"Are you sure about that?" I asked.

"I'm certain," Redman said. "That woman you're dreaming about is worth more than sixty seconds. Besides, if you can't handle the tunnel for sixty seconds, you're probably goin' to Georgia. You got two powerful reasons to handle sixty seconds in that hole. You can do it."

"I guess I can."

"I know damn well you can," he said.

I knew he was right. I could endure that for Claire. I didn't even think about Georgia. She's what I craved.

"Here, this is for you," he said.

"What is it?"

"Open the bag," he said.

"Is this corn whiskey?"

"Yes."

"I don't even like that stuff."

"You keep it. You may want a shot of this stuff just as you're going into the tunnel."

"What place am I in order to go out?" I asked.

"Third place. Wes is first, I am second, and then you are third. You won't have to worry about anybody holding you back. We want to get out of there as bad as you do, maybe more. We'll be flyin'. We'll be smokin' ass to get through."

For the first time, I felt very good about the tunnel and the whole plan. I knew my friends and knew they were good men. I'd have to work to even keep up with them. I did not need to worry — they'd be smokin' ass.

Chapter 10

For the first time since my enlistment, I did not think about Claire. I now managed to think only of the tunnel and escape. I knew the claustrophobia would test me, but exactly how much it would test me I did not know, and I was not frightened. Strangely, a calmness came over me as I realized the struggle would only be for sixty seconds. I felt a strong confidence from the excitement of freedom.

My friends would be waiting at the entrance of the tunnel, and I would rather be early than late meeting them. As I arrived, Charles Redman and John Wesley Williams were ready and waiting for me. Wes quickly entered the tunnel and was gone. It made me feel strong.

"I'll give him about two minutes and then I'll go," Redman said. "Remember to keep low and keep moving. Whatever you do, Ezra, you must keep movin'."

I nodded to him but did not speak. Suddenly, he was in the tunnel and gone. I was alone, but I was ready. I had waited a long time for this moment. I was ready.

The soil in the tunnel was strangely moist. I had expected the ground to be dry, even dusty, but it was not. The tunnel was completely dark, yet the three of us were not deterred. I knew the tunnel was not long, and if I kept low and crawled steadily, I would be okay. I dug my fingers in the earth and threw small bits of dirt behind me as I edged forward.

"Keep low, keep crawling," I kept telling myself. I had experienced no claustrophobia, but then about halfway through the tunnel, it happened.

I banged my head on the tunnel ceiling and realized I must stay low as I crawled. A second time I bumped the ceiling, and I panicked.

"Stay low, stay low," I kept saying.

Despite my panicking, I kept low and kept crawling. I realized I must be halfway through the tunnel and I must keep digging with my fingers.

"Dear God," I prayed. "Please don't let there be any cave-in from this ceiling." I guess it was the most powerful prayer I'd ever uttered and probably the shortest.

I thought I heard a voice as I kept crawling. Again, I heard a voice. "What the hell could that be," I said out loud. I wondered if someone was trapped in the tunnel in front of me. Again I heard that voice. At last I understood. The voice was from Redman as Wes was pulling him out of the tunnel, and they were calling for me.

I crawled as hard as I could and thought my heart would burst. I was close to the end and knew that nothing would stop me now. There were only a few feet left, and at last, I could see them.

I held out my hands, and both of them pulled me steadily out of the tomb. I scraped my hip on my left side, and it burned greatly. It was probably bleeding badly inside my pants, but no matter — in a few seconds, I would be free. My friends pulled hard, and I was free from that tunnel at last.

"Thank you, Jesus," I said. "Thank you, Jesus."

The three of us made a sharp left turn and headed west, out of Virginia and into the mountains of West Virginia. This feeling of freedom left me light-headed, almost intoxicated. Yet I knew I could not be careless and stray from our course.

We found an abandoned road heading west, and we ran steadily on it. Branches from both sides of the road lashed our faces, but at least they gave us cover as we traveled. Probably in another year, the small branches of the trees would completely cover the road, but we didn't worry about that now. This little road was perfect for us, and we traveled several miles and hoped that Confederate Virginia was behind us.

West Virginia was now Union and should be helpful to us. My planning had been correct. We saw no other men and presumed that most of our comrades had headed straight north, not west as we were traveling.

"Wait," said Wes.

"Wait for what?" I asked.

"Don't you hear it?" asked Wes.

"Hear what? What the hell are you talking about?" I asked.

"I think I hear dogs," said Redman.

"Yes, you do," said Wes.

"Dogs?" I asked

"Yes," said Wes. "I thought I heard them a while back — now I'm sure."

"Maybe they're a local farmer's dogs," I said.

"Let's keep running. If we continue to hear them, we'll know there are hounds following us," said Wes.

The three of us picked up the pace and hoped to put more distance between ourselves and our imaginary pursuers. We ran steadily but now knew we would not be able to keep up this pace. Our time in incarceration at Libby had left us in weak condition with little endurance.

"I need to rest," said Redman. "I can't go on without a break. Let's just stop for a few minutes."

We listened for the dogs and were not happy.

"I can hear them," said Wes. "There's no doubt they're getting louder, and they're growing closer."

"We've got to decide what to do," I said.

"What *can* we do?" asked Redman.

"We can do three things," I said. "We can continue on this road, and they'll surely be on us soon. We can split up and hope this confuses them."

"And what is this third thing?" asked Redman.

"We can kill the lead dog," I said. "The lead dog is always the alpha, or leader of the pack. If we kill him, the others will probably scatter."

"What in hell do you mean, kill him?" asked Wes. "All I have is a small pocket knife I stole from Libby."

Redman picked up a sturdy branch from the ground. The branch was oak and several inches thick.

"This should do it," he said. "This is plenty strong."

"I don't think I've got the stomach for it," said Wes. "I'm sorry, I just can't do it."

"I'll do it," said Redman. "I'm not going back to Libby or any other prison. I'm not going back, and that's all there is to it."

The three of us hid behind a large multiflora rose bush. Redman stood closest to the old road, and Wes and I stood behind him.

"How are you going to do it?" asked Wes.

"I'm going to try to break his back," answered Redman. "It's going to be pretty messy, but I'll get it done. I hope one blow will be enough. And everyone else be quiet — not another word!"

We could hear the dogs clearly now. They were probably only a hundred feet away. Their barking was loud and clear. In less than sixty seconds, they would confront us.

We could see them now and hoped they couldn't see us. There were four of them — long-eared hounds. The leader came directly through the front of the rosebush, where Redman swung the heavy branch. The dog gave a terrible scream; it was awful. He swung the limb a second time, and the large hound was silent. It was that second blow that silenced him. The other three dogs turned and raced back down the old road.

For a short while, we didn't speak — or probably we couldn't speak, especially Redman. It was a gruesome experience, but it had to be done.

"Let's go," said Wes. "Let's go, Redman. Now! We gotta go and go now!"

Redman didn't answer but shook his head up and down. It was obvious he was overcoming his grief.

We ran steadily up the old road, slowly at first, but steadily and then a little faster. After about a mile, we decided to pull up and rest.

Since we had no compass and no map, we had no idea where the state line was that separated Virginia from West Virginia. Hungry and exhausted, we staggered along in the semi-darkness as if we were inebriated. The cold, the dogs, and the tiredness would not stop us. We kept up a steady pace, as if we were almost uncontrollable. It seemed we were almost predestined by our Creator to put one foot in front of the other. We would not stop again for another two hours, but I pictured in my mind that in a few days we would cross the River and head into Ohio — and Claire.

More than the cold or the mountains, we dreaded the Rebel patrols that searched for runaway slaves. The patrols also received awards if they brought back escaped Union soldiers. The night was cold, but somehow we managed to sleep soundly, probably from our exhaustion.

The sun at last broke over the horizon, but we stayed in our shelter, a small valley of large Scotch pine trees. Although daylight broke, we needed more rest. We had not spoken since we had encountered the dogs, and at last, Redman spoke: "Ezra, did you remember to bring that whiskey?" he asked.

"Damn! I forgot it," I said.

"Do you remember where it is?" asked Wes.

"It's no use. I left it under my bunk at Libby," I said. "Someone will find it, and they're welcome to it. There's no point in worrying about that whiskey now."

The three of us sat quietly in the pines and devoured some red apples from a farmer's tree. Wes stood and motioned with his hand for Redman and me to follow. We rose and headed west, farther into the mountains. We moved slowly, for we were still tired, and our muscles had grown soft from months of confinement. We trekked on in our arduous journey, always traveling west by northwest. The sun was high now and very warm. We started down a long hill and directly in front of us was a small creek.

"Look!" exclaimed Wes. From the other side of the hill was smoke. It obviously came from a good-sized fire, but was it a campfire or a home?

"We need to get some food from some folks, if it's a home," I said. "But if it's a home, is it Union or Rebel?"

"There's only one way to find out," said Redman. "We've got to get down this hill and follow the smoke on the other side."

"The two of you wait here," I said. "I'll work my way slowly around the hill, and whatever I find, I'll be back."

The woods were not thick and for the first time on our journey, the walking was easy. I could see most of the house, but no one was out. I looked closely for a dog that kept watch, but there was none. I crept closer, alert for a hidden dog.

In front of the house was a large limb from a tree that served as a flagpole. On the pole flew our flag. My eyes filled with tears, and I quickly wiped them away. As I returned to my comrades, a great wave of peace came over me. How long it had been since I had felt such peace, I could not remember.

"There's a flag flying in their front yard," I said to my friends.

"Is it stars and stripes or stars and bars?" asked Wes.

"Stars and stripes."

"Hallelujah!" shouted Redman. "Thank God for big favors. We are free at last."

We knocked on the door, and an attractive woman opened it. We undoubtedly looked very strange to her, but we didn't care.

"Ma'am," I said, "we are Union officers who escaped from Libby Prison in Richmond, Virginia. We are trying to get back to Ohio and saw your flag."

"You men are welcome," she said. "We are the MacDowell family, and you may come in."

"Thank you, ma'am, but we were hoping you could spare some food for our journey."

"You have supper with us tonight. I imagine it has been a good while since you have had a home-cooked, sit-down dinner."

"Bless you, ma'am," I said. "Can you tell me which state of the Union we are in?" I asked.

"You have reached the Mountain State, West Virginia," she said.

"Thank you," the three of us said simultaneously.

That night we ate roast pork, fried potatoes, mixed vegetables and fresh bread. It was a feast, and we left nothing on our plates. I had not had a meal like this since my mother's after-church Sunday dinner before my enlistment – three-and-a-half years ago. Later we bedded down in their small barn. We covered ourselves with the blankets Mrs. MacDowell had lent us. After being covered with the blankets, we dug deep into the hay. It was soft and warm. We slept soundly, as if we were a thousand miles from Libby.

* * * * *

The following morning we headed on our way, north by northwest. The MacDowells gave us some fruit and bread with pieces of pork from last night's supper.

"Keep the sun at your back and head west," said Mr. MacDowell. "In about four or five miles, you'll find a swift-moving stream that heads north. This stream is not very wide, but it's deep. Careful not to cross it."

"If it goes north, where does it end?" I asked.

"If you turn to your right, as it heads north, it should take you all the way to the Ohio River. I'm pretty certain it empties into the Ohio. The forest is pretty thick, but you should make it."

"Thank you for the food and all your help," said Wes.

"You're welcome."

"God bless you," I said.

We headed on our journey westward and then north. We were confident and knew our task ahead. After about an hour, we found the stream, turned right and followed it, heading north. We had no idea how far the Great River was ahead, but it didn't matter. It was the last part of our journey that lay ahead.

Chapter 11

I began to think more and more about my two comrades. I had realized for some time how fortunate I was to have two worthy young men traveling and escaping with me. From time to time I thought about them, but perhaps the strain of the journey kept me from dwelling on them very much. I realized now that I never would've escaped or made it this far without them.

Wes was a good-hearted soul, pleasant and often-times jovial. He was a son of a clergyman and was very serious about his tasks. Despite his pleasantness, there was a toughness about him that was easy to admire. He was not quarrelsome, but when he was pushed, he was a formidable young man. If a conflict ever arose between two groups of men, I would be very happy that Wes was on my side. I had never seen him in a physical struggle, but I'm quite sure he would be a strong opponent.

I did not know what Wes had done in civilian life but had the feeling that whatever it was, he would be successful. Whatever path he chose, it was easy to have confidence that his word would be kept and he could be strongly relied on. I knew from other conversations that he had an older and a younger brother, and the three of them all seemed to have characteristics of courage and accountability. I was glad he was my friend and glad his commitment to return to Ohio was the same as mine.

Charles Redman was somewhat of a contradiction. He was a practical man with mechanical skills. It seemed there were very few things that he couldn't make or repair. He also was an ideal companion to have in your group for any journey like our own.

At the same time, Redman was a scholar. He was a learned man who had studied two years at Ohio Wesleyan and had planned to return to Wesleyan after the war. In a rather short time, he had the ability to evaluate an issue better than the rest of us. I cannot remember any time that he had an opinion that Wes and I didn't concur with and understand him. I was a blessed guy to have such strong comrades.

The sun was bright and gave some light, but the air was cold, very cold. By midmorning the sun would warm the air but not just yet. We oftentimes hid during the day and traveled at night, but we were no longer fearful of traveling in the daylight. Since visiting with the MacDowells, we knew we were traveling through friendly country. We wanted to reach the Ohio River before dusk, and we grew bolder as we headed west and north.

We still surveyed everything before we moved along the creek. We did not want to rush into any problems after all our struggle.

We heard a noise ever so soft directly in front of us, approximately 150 feet in front of us. Then the sound was gone. The three of us crouched low in the high grass. Only our breathing could be heard, and after a short wait, we could hear that same noise again in front of us. We waited and listened.

We were in Union territory but still had our fears about a Confederate patrol. We looked hard for gray uniforms but saw nothing. We hid a long time; we were anxious to move north yet controlled our anxiety. We had come too far now to fail. What would we do if we were confronted by armed patrol? We had no guns, so we kept low, very low.

To my right, I noticed Redman moving very slowly, then motioning with his hand for us to come to him. I kept low in the grass and crawled to him. We were still fearful of a Rebel slave-catching patrol. We had heard in Libby that the Confederacy had kept men in western Virginia to catch escaping slaves near the River.

I froze halfway toward Redman. I was terrified that we were moving directly into trouble. Redman now was crawling toward me. He had obviously grown tired of waiting for me to come to him. It appeared my two companions were as much afraid of a patrol as I was.

"Why did you stop?" asked Redman.

"There is something directly in our path," I whispered. "Can't you hear it? I stopped before we were seen. I thought it might be a Confederate patrol."

Wes had now joined us. "I don't think it is," he said.

"How do you know that?" I asked.

"Because I can see it," said Wes. "It's a deer."

"It's what?" said Redman.

"It's a deer," said Wes again. "It's been in front of us for some time. I was certain that you could see it. That's why I didn't motion to you."

"I still don't see it." I said.

"Just to the right of that large dark tree. I think the tree is a big red oak," said Wes. "Can't you see it? Ezra, you must be blind."

"I see it now," said Redman. "It's a doe — a very large doe — just to the right of that dark tree."

"That's her," said Wes. "She's been hanging around for some reason, and she's directly in our path."

"If we move slowly, she won't panic but simply wander off," I said.

We stood motionless and could easily see her now. We hoped the wind was in our favor, and she couldn't get our scent. Motionless in the high grass, it didn't appear that she could see us.

Quietly the three of us walked toward her. Her head quickly turned toward us. Her tail began to twitch nervously.

"You said that she'd walk away," said Wes.

"She will. Just keep moving slowly toward her and don't make any quick movements," I said.

The deer trotted slowly toward our right with her tail up like a white flag. We waited. There was no doubt that she saw us now. It was actually a relief that she moved on.

"Why has she hung around here so long? She seems to want to stay," said Redman. "Can you guys tell me why she stayed?"

"Could be a fawn," I said. "Keep moving. We won't have any time to explore."

I could see tracks from the doe. I pulled back two large ferns and could now see beneath them. It was her fawn, and she had not wanted to leave it. The fawn huddled tightly and made itself as small as it could. The large white spots on it were easy to see now. Its rump was wet, and it had clearly been born within the last hour. It was a beautiful sight and a good omen for us, but we could not linger.

I stood for only a few seconds and didn't motion to either Redman or Wes. I would tell them later because we need to leave this place before the doe returned. We moved on.

* * * * *

The sun was warmer now and almost directly over us. It was noonday, and the air was no longer cool. My two comrades had moved directly in front of me and had stopped at a small apple tree. The apples were small and might not be very tasty, but I stopped with them, and we decided to carry as many as we could. Many apples were on the ground, and we gathered as many as we had room for. Some obviously had worms in them. No matter, we gathered them anyway. After we cleared the ground, we started pulling them off all the branches we could reach.

We still didn't know how far we had to go, so we stuffed as many in our pockets as we could. We ate them as we walked and were not particular. We avoided the bruises and worm spots as best we could but were not always successful. Yet the size of our apple feast raised our spirits. We had eaten very little since we left the MacDowells. We pressed on. We never had enough food, but we kept moving north.

On our left side, to the west, I could hear the flow of water. The stream couldn't be the Ohio because it flowed north and west. I called my comrades.

"If we're careful, we might find some fish near this river," I said. "But we must be careful."

"We haven't heard any gunfire in four or five days," said Redman. "Maybe the Rebs have pulled south. Maybe Grant is moving on Richmond. What do you think, Ezra?"

"Could be," I said. "I think the best sign is that we've heard no gunfire. I think the Rebs have moved south."

"If we come to any river, we need to stay on this side of it and in the trees. We shouldn't show ourselves," said Redman. "I wish to hell I had a rifle, but I'd settle for a Remington revolver."

"I wouldn't count on that," I said. "If we're going to wish, I wish we had three good horses and three rifles."

"Well, I can wish, can't I?" said Redman.

"If you're gonna wish, wish each of us had a carbine and a revolver — and maybe a sword thrown in also," said Wes.

"Let's stop all this gabbin' about guns and horses and make our way to the river," I said. "Perhaps we'll find something we can use ahead. That would be nice."

The sun was very hot now, and we steadily pressed forward. We heard the river and then we could smell it and then we could see it. We stood behind the bushes and would not show ourselves. It was not a large river, and we saw no one on either bank. A small wooden boat was tied to a small tree at the bank of the river. We looked at each other. Should we go down and examine the boat?

"Once we show ourselves, it might be too late," I said.

"We could use that boat to row north. It would help a lot because the current would be with us," said Wes.

"I don't like that," said Redman.

"I don't like it either," I said. "We'd be vulnerable on that water if anyone moved up on us. We'll be moving a lot slower on the land but safer. I just don't like it."

"Maybe we could just look around the boat for anything," said Redman. "If we move carefully, we should be fine."

The boat had nothing inside it, but behind the little craft, we found a small treasure. Two fishing poles and a thick staff were near the river.

"What's on that little staff?" I asked.

We pulled up the line tied to the staff, and Wes pulled hard, and at last we saw. It was a treasure — an absolutely small treasure that we could carry.

"Damn," said Redman. "It's a stringer of fish. Look, there're three, four — five of them!"

"Thank God for small favors," said Wes.

"That's the truth," I said. "Let's go. Pick up the poles and fish. Untie the boat and let it go upstream."

"Why?" asked Wes. "Why not just leave them here?"

"If they are all gone, they will think someone went north on the little river. Maybe they won't look on land. There is a good chance they are Union folks anyway," I said. "Come on. Let's go and don't forget to push the boat free and bring those fish."

Since we had left Libby, we had been blessed with very good weather. Some of the nights were a little cool, but the weather had basically been warm and no rain. At last our luck had changed, and the heavens opened. It rained steadily and very hard. It wasn't long until we were entirely soaked. Every portion of our clothing was wet, and there was nothing we could do. There was no point in hiding under some trees because we were already saturated.

"We might have fish tonight, but it's going to be a while before we can dry out everything," said Wes. "I don't care how long it takes. I want fish tonight."

We started north again with several hours of daylight left for us. We were very tired, but our spirits were high with our new food.

"Ezra, are we gonna clean these fish now to cook if this rain ever stops?" asked Redman. "I am mighty hungry."

"I'm starved," said Wes.

"We can start now and get a little farther north away from this river if we keep going," I said.

We continued north following the little river, and the rain continued. We found some large stones and knew it was a good place to clean the fish. Suddenly the rain stopped as quickly as it had started.

"Look on the ground," I said. "Look on the ground for any dry sticks, leaves or dead branches under those pine trees. There branches probably keep things dry underneath."

After a short while, we managed to get a small fire burning. We nurtured it along carefully, feeding it with dry leaves and sticks. Wes came back from a journey with a pile of dry branches and carefully placed them on the little fire which was burning well now.

We held the fish on small sticks just over the fire. The edges of each fish burned slightly, but we didn't care. The burnt skin added to the flavor of each filet. The white filet pulled loose from the spine and was sweet. We pulled away the tiny bones, but if they were very soft we ate them also. It was wonderful.

"Don't move," whispered Redman. "There's something moving to our left. Whatever it is, I don't think it's seen our fire. Can you see what it is, Ezra?"

"No."

"I see him now," said Wes. "He's not very tall, and I think he's a black man, probably a runaway slave. He's coming right at us."

"Let him come in," I said.

We watched closely as the Black showed no fear of us. Steadily and directly, he came to what was left of our fire.

"Mastah," said the African. "May I have a piece of your food? I am powerful hungry, with nothing for two days."

"You may have a piece of our fish, but I'm not your master. You have no master."

"What shall I call you?" asked the black man.

"Call me 'sir' or 'mister,'" I said. We gave him three apples, and Wes gave him two small pieces of fish.

"Thank you for the food, especially the fish."

"Where are ya headed?" asked Wes. "Are you running away? Where are you from?"

"I left Claiborne County, Tennessee, five days ago," said the black man. "I'm headed for Cincinnata, I can find friends there."

"Are you planning to travel with us?" asked Redman.

"No," he blurted out. "I've done alright by myself so far. The larger the group, the easier it is for someone to spot us. I ain't seen a single gray coat in Kentucky, and there ain't no Rebel soldiers here."

"Maybe not, but there are some mercenaries," I said. "These men will send you back if they can catch you. You're a smart man. You don't wanna be caught after you've come so far."

"They might also shoot us," said Wes. "They can claim we're abolitionists helping you. You're right — you're better off without us."

"Sir, how do I git to Cincinnata?"

"After you cross the River, go left," said Wes. "Go left as the sun goes down. It's on the other side of the River, the north side, and it's a long way. You'll find it — just follow the River west."

We watched the African disappear into the woods north of us and knew if he got to Cincinnati, he would find help. We had heard he could find help in Ripley but weren't sure.

We finished all the fish and put out the fire. We were very tired, and no one wanted to go on, and so we slept there for the night in the deep grass. I felt guilty telling the African to go on without us, but it was probably better for him and for us. A larger group would be easier for someone to spot and easier for them to trail. We had made the right decision. Nothing was going to keep us from getting to the River and nothing was going to stop me from getting back to Claire.

Chapter 12

We had no idea how far we had traveled, but we were a little hungry and a little tired. We knew we were on course for we had traveled alongside the small stream that Mr. MacDowell had described. The sun was high, almost directly above, and so we guessed it was around the noon hour.

"Let's stop," said Wes. "It's a good time to eat."

"Good idea," I said. "We can eat the last of the food the MacDowells gave to us."

"After we eat, I wouldn't mind a short nap," said Redman. "I'm wearin' out faster than I thought I would."

"Let's make it only a short nap," I said. "I don't want to keep her waiting any longer than necessary."

We ate our food very slowly because we didn't know when our next meal would be. We wasted nothing and ate every crumb. It was easy to fall asleep. The sun was not very warm and helped us to sleep soundly. We slept several hours longer than we wanted, but the way we slept showed us we obviously needed the rest.

We picked up our few belongings and headed north, the stream always on our left. Mr. MacDowell had been correct — the woods were thick as we kept close to the stream. Two houses were across the stream, and we were tempted to cross over and inquire about some food, but we didn't. We knew we would pass farms ahead and hoped most of them would be on our side of the stream.

It was obvious now that we would not reach the Ohio River this day. The sun was half covered by the horizon and in a short while would be completely down. We all felt where we were would be as good as any spot to spend the night. We began to find branches and small logs to start a fire. We were confident that no Confederate patrols or agents would be this far north. The fire was wonderful for us. Except for the fireplace at the MacDowell house, it was the first time we'd felt the flames of a close fire in nearly two years. I stood only a few inches from the flames, and the wind blew the heat almost directly on me. At times it almost burnt me, yet I didn't move away from our little hearth in the forest.

"You guys can sit next to that fire all night, but I'm going to sleep," said Redman. "Wake me in the morning. Good night."

"Good night," answered Wes.

For a long time, Wes and I sat in silence. We placed some dried branches and two small logs on the fire. We stared at the flames, almost hypnotized by them. The wood crackled in the fire and even the sound of it was sweet to us. There was an endless supply of branches, logs and leaves around us, and so we were able to keep our little campfire burning all night if we could keep awake to feed it more fuel.

For perhaps the first time, we realized how far we had journeyed. The cold dismal nights of Libby were long-gone now, and we could see that the road to the River began the last trek of our journey.

"You think about her a lot, don't you?" asked Wes.

"Only about ten or twelve times a day," I said, smiling at him. "Now that we're closer to the River, I think about her even more."

"We've been gone almost three years. Don't you think she might've changed her mind?" said Wes. "You don't seem to worry about that."

"No, not at all. There's a deep understanding between us. She's lovely, but to me, she's more beautiful on the inside. That may sound strange to you, but that's how it feels to me. It's a little difficult to explain."

"I think I understand," said Wes.

"How about you? Who do you think of?"

"About my parents and my younger brother. I have a sweetheart also, but I've not known her as long as you've known Clarinda. But I think things will work out." We stopped our conversation, and again we sat in silence, gazing at the fire. We grew tired but somehow didn't wish to desert the heat.

"It's time," said Wes.

I knew what he meant. It was time to sleep. But before we turned in, Wes placed as much wood on the fire as he could. We were certain it wouldn't last until dawn, but it should last several hours, giving us some heat and light.

* * * * *

Since we had no pocket watch, we didn't know the time when we arose. The sun was up only a short time, and there was enough light for us to again head north toward the Ohio. The day was pleasant and warm, and by the middle of the day, the sun was very warm.

Redman placed his finger over his lips, and instantly we knew he wanted us to be silent. We crouched lower to the ground and strained hard to see what Redman had seen, but we saw nothing. Slowly I shook my head from side to side, indicating that I had seen nothing. Again he put his fingers to his lips for us to be silent. Wes and I strained hard but could see or hear nothing. I grew frustrated and doubted if Redman had really seen anything — maybe he was hallucinating. After a few minutes, he moved his fingers from his lips and pointed to our left. At that minute, I could see someone walking. It appeared to be that same black runaway slave we had seen several days earlier. We stood motionless and let him come toward us. When he was only about twenty feet from us, Wes spoke. "Don't run, black man! We do not pursue you. In fact, we'll help you cross the River."

The runaway was startled and obviously afraid but didn't run.

"Join us if you wish," I said. "We probably have another day in our journey to reach the river. You probably will be safer to travel with us."

The black man was no longer afraid or edgy, but he did not directly join us. I didn't care if he joined us or traveled by himself, and I told him this. He joined us, and the four of us headed north. The runaway said nothing, but it was obvious that he remembered us and preferred our company since we only had a short distance left to reach the River.

Three hours later, as darkness fell, we reached the Ohio River. We could hear the river and even smell it before we saw it steadily moving west, heading toward the Mississippi. For a short while, we stared at it with a great inner feeling of satisfaction. We found some large bushes under which we would spend the night. We would cross the River in the morning.

Chapter 13

We walked on the pebbles located at the edge of the River. The pebbles were not sharp but were worn smooth from the constant movement of the River. Even though they were small, they didn't cause any pain to our bare feet. We stared across the River to the other side in Ohio. It was much farther than we had imagined. No one took lightly the swim we had before us. We knew the River was cold, the current was fairly strong, and none of us was excited about immediately crossing.

"I dreamt about this last night," said Wes.

"You dreamt about us crossing the River last night?" I asked.

"No. I dreamt about us standing on these pebbles and looking across."

"You're joking," I said. "Why would you dream about these pebbles?"

"I dreamt of us standing here and looking across to the other side. It reminded me of the Israelites looking upon the Promised Land."

Our black comrade began to walk into the water. He walked farther and farther and now the water was up to his chest. He looked back at us and waved. Then he turned away from us and began the long task of swimming across.

"Good luck," we said. He knew the way to Cincinnati, and we were certain that when he reached the other side, he would head down the far bank toward the great city. I was happy for him and yet a little sad. We would probably never see him again.

"When should we try?" asked Redman. "If we wait a few hours, the sun will certainly be warmer."

"Whenever the two of you wish to go is fine with me," I said.

Wes walked to the edge of the stones, where the water lapped at them. "I think I want to go now," he said. "I don't want to wait any longer. You two can wait if you wish, but for me, the time has come."

"Do you think we could build a raft?" asked Redman.

"What do you think about that, Ezra?" asked Wes.

"I don't think so."

"I'm not sure I can swim that far," said Redman.

"It'll take us hours to build anything," I said. "I don't think we can build it anyway. We'd have to find logs and some kind of rope or vines. We have no oars or paddles, no rudder — the River will just take us farther downstream toward Indiana."

"Maybe we could each take a small log," said Redman.

"It would take energy from us to propel the log as well as ourselves," said Wes.

"He's right," I said. "Swimming is going to be the best and the quickest."

"That damn water will almost be freezin', and what if I can't make it?" said Redman.

"Just swim slowly and think of how far we've already come," I said.

"Do you remember Libby?" asked Wes. "Do you remember the tunnel, the forest and everything else we've had to overcome? Remember all those things, and you'll do it," Wes said firmly.

We tied our shoes around our necks and headed into the River. We moved slowly at first and then began to swim. We swam steadily and tried not to waste any energy.

"Be bold," I said. "We've come too far to let anything hold us back now."

Slowly the Ohio side of the River seemed to grow closer. We swam steadily. Several logs passed us in the River, and we were careful not to let them strike us; we let them pass us and swam on. We did not speak to each other and conserved all the energy we could. I tried not to think about the distance. It seemed like we had passed the halfway point, but I didn't want to think about that and continued to swim steadily.

My feet could touch something on the bottom now, and I thought I could probably walk the last sixty or seventy feet. We tried to walk the distance, but the current was too strong. It almost forced us over, and we began to swim again.

Wes slowly passed me, but Redman still swam behind. I turned and could see him, but I didn't want to take any energy away from my swimming. I worried he would lose his strength, but he kept coming slowly and then I no longer worried. Again I could touch the bottom. It seemed like a long sand bar that came out from the shore. I walked slowly, afraid that I might step in a gigantic hole, but I didn't. At last I realized — we had done it! We had done it! We walked steadily on the sand bar. When we reached the pebbles on the far side, we began to stagger from exhaustion. But the water was shallow, and we hadn't much farther to go.

The water only reached our knees now, and we stumbled along on the pebbles to the grass that lay ahead. We breathed heavily, but at last we knew we were safe.

The air was cold, but the morning sun had come out from behind the clouds, and we could feel some of its warmth. I don't remember how long we lay on the grass, but slowly the sun over-came our chill, and we almost fell asleep in the grass. Thank God for the sun!

We found a small path that headed directly north away from the grass and the River. The little path widened and took us to a road that had tracks from wagon wheels.

"Let's take it," said Wes. "As long as it heads north, we'll be fine."

"Let's be certain that it stays north with no bends or changes in direction," said Redman.

Our clothes began to dry as the sun climbed higher and grew warmer. We could no longer see the River behind us as we continued north on the dirt road.

Chapter 14

We walked steadily — not very fast, but steadily. The sun was high now, very warm, and even comforting. Our clothes were totally dry, and all the thoughts of the River were far behind us.

"You think we should head for home or report to our armory or at least to some armory?" asked Redman.

"I'm not exactly sure what to do," I said. "I think I want to go home first and then go to the armory later. They're not going to fuss about time as long as we report in sometime."

"I'm going home first," said Wes.

"So am I," I answered. "They can wait a short time for us. We've waited a long time for this day."

"I don't want to get into some trouble," said Redman.

"Trouble! What the hell do you think we've been in for the last three years?"

"I didn't mean the fighting," said Redman. "I don't want us to be breakin' some army regulation."

"I don't give a damn about any regulation," said Wes. "I'm going home first, and that's all there is to it."

"It probably would be better if the three of us reported in together," I answered.

"Then that's what we'll do," said Redman. "After we have each gone home, we'll meet up together and go to our home armory. We can make up three days after we get home and then report in."

We must've walked eight or ten miles when we heard a strange sound behind us. After turning to look behind, we saw an approaching farmer with two black horses pulling his wagon. It was a welcome sight, and we stopped. We didn't have to wait very long for him to be upon us.

"Can we catch a ride with you, partner?" I asked. "We have walked a long way and need a little help."

"Sure can. I'm only going to Chillicothe to deliver my baskets of fruit to market, but you're welcome to go that far," he said.

We thanked him and climbed on board the old wagon. The road was bumpy, but we were happy with any ride we could get — anything that would deliver us from walking.

"Help yourself to a piece of fruit from those baskets," said the farmer.

The apples were good, the peaches were better, and the juicy pears were wonderful. We gorged on the fruit and put a few pieces in our pockets. We wanted to save some for later. Some miles later, the farmer turned onto a road on the right. It was the road to Chillicothe.

"If you three want to go north, you want to get off now. You don't want to go to Chillicothe," he said.

"What's the next town going north?" I asked. "What should we look for?"

"You want to go to Circleville, and after that, keep on this road north. There will be some signs."

"What's the next big town north of Circleville?" asked Redman.

"Columbus," said the farmer. "I think that's where you want to go."

"That's where we want to go," I said. "That's where we want to go. We won't need any road signs then."

"Good luck to you, men."

"Thanks."

"I hope we get another ride," said Redman.

"So do I," said Wes. "This has been one hell of a journey. I sure would hate to have to make it again."

"So would I," I said. Then I turned to my comrades and smiled. "But if I had to, I guess I could."

We continued north toward Circleville.

Chapter 15

Ten days after my arrival home, the community had a wonderful homecoming celebrating my return. It was on a Sunday following worship at the Wharton Methodist Church. Every single relative of mine came that day. Every friend I had came to be with us — farm friends from Wharton, Forest, Upper Sandusky, Findlay and Bucyrus. The church overflowed that morning, and many chairs were placed outside the windows of the sanctuary so that those who couldn't get inside were able to hear the service. Half of the hymnals from inside the sanctuary were given to those who sat outside, and those who remained inside shared Bibles and hymnals. Our closing hymn was "The Battle Hymn of the Republic."

The weather was perfect that day, as if those in heaven had made it that way for us. Our dinner after the service was the largest I'd ever seen, and for the first time, I realized how many people loved me and how many had prayed for my safe return. The day was filled with joy. Our community, our state and the nation was joyous over the end of the conflict. The height of the celebration was something that probably many of us would never experience again. It would be years before the nation's wounds would be healed, but in our celebration, like many throughout the land, would be a beginning.

Claire and I managed to steal away for a few minutes. I held her and kissed her the way I had kissed her on that Sunday before I left with the Ohio Volunteers. I held her and then kissed her again.

Chapter 16

My period of enlistment was three years and was to end on September 24, 1865. Fortunately, the war ended before that, and I was honorably discharged from the 123rd Ohio Volunteers and the Grand Army of the Republic on June 12, 1865. I put away my beautiful blue dress uniform and my silver lieutenant's bars. Only once thereafter did I take them out and relive some old memories. I left them to the next generation of my family to have them and reminisce about the past.

On November 8, 1865, I married my sweetheart, Clarinda A. Jackson. There were many days during the conflict that I doubted I would ever see her again, but thank God in heaven, I survived.

One year later, in December 1866, our son, Henry Jackson Van Buren, was born. His middle name was taken from Clarinda's maiden name, and he was the heir that continued our family's name into the next century.

The following year, in 1867, I lost my beloved Claire in childbirth, along with my baby daughter. I had her only two years, but I am certain that my memories of her and my love for her sustained me in the bitter years of the War Between the States, and I thank God for her.

* * * * *

Ezra Hezekiah Van Buren died on December 10, 1915, at the age of 73. He is buried in Wharton Cemetery in Wharton, Ohio.